Fingerprints on the Heart

A Story Written by Shiloh Gastello

To my mentors, Michael and Victoria Terra, who re-enlivened and nurtured my love of writing. To my parents, John and Melba Gastello, who started me on my writing journey. Thank you for helping me to become a better version of myself.

Introduction

Let me paint you a picture, spin you a tale. This is a story of how a traveler learned from a child. These are the meanderings that were part of processing the love, loss, realizations, and deep introspections of a life. They are a record of appreciating the lessons life teaches us all. This story is an exploration of how we all find home.

Is home a place, or a mindset? Sometimes home isn't a place, but something you find in people. In that sense, home is both where we've been and where we are going next. Who we plant seeds with and how long we water them. Each person teaches you something new, and that's why it can hurt more when you leave them. Because people gain more meaning for us as we move forward. That means that it was worth our time together. Hold that dear because that, in a way, is home.

This story is a record of a traveler's journey exploring the space between the subconscious and conscious parts of his mind and memories. After all, what is a time machine but a vessel, a mind propelling back through lessons learned throughout life? This is a record of the lessons learned from a man who remembered a boy's heart. They are one and the same.

Part 1

The Boy

I

The Boy and The Time Machine

"Wait…where am I?" The boy exclaimed. With the fervor of summer curiosity burning his brow, he raised himself with sleepy determination. Finding his ground, he realized he was in Kentucky. "Was I dreaming? Here once more. It's been years. This is where I first began to heal inside. Why am I back here? To finish healing? Well, by the grief of mercy, I will be completely alive now even if it kills me."

The boy remembered the old, dusty chair in the cold, wet closet. "Didn't Dad say that if you remember something hard enough when sitting in that chair, you will find yourself face to face with it?" In his mind's eye, he saw the chair now—it spoke of the future-present, a time of lingering nows that were somehow of another time. This ever-moving, non-linear pathway was said to whisper lessons that were once forgotten. It spoke of lessons learned on summer nights when the smell of dandelion wine moved through the air as thick as a potent memory. It was steel in the mouth, thick and bitter, yet oddly sweet enough to make you cry. The hot wind of summer hit his memories. He closed his eyes, soaking them in for a moment before opening them.

The boy found himself walking on pavement. Glancing to the side, he noticed something…no, someone, moving around the corner. He saw the shape of a woman, lonely and afraid. She did not speak. Turning to face the boy, she began moving toward him; each step launched fear into his chest. This emotion was hot and feverish. As he took a quick gulp of air, the fear of death and life converged into one crystalline moment. Suddenly, he knew he was not safe. In fact, he never had been. At least, not as long as "she" was there. Her "presence" was intoxicating and misunderstood, yet empathetic.

He called out to her, "Hey! Do you need help?"

No answer came back to him. A night bird cawed. Suddenly, the woman shifted her weight and began to run toward him. The boy ran. The night ran. The shadows ran with them all in a blur.

As he rounded the corner of the block on this warm summer night that felt as cold as a Kentucky winter, he entered the shadows. He became shrouded by them, hiding him from the gaze of the woman who sought to reach him. He turned around to face her, but she was gone. Nothing of her remained except her thinly-veiled presence. Had she actually been there? Was she a figment? Or even worse, a memory trying to resurface? His heart jumped in his throat but then he found his nerve, and checked around the corner again. She was there once more, staring at him with a longing expression as warm and inviting as a sunset about to end too soon. He could feel her breath in his throat. It was his breath too. Was she also him?

With each quiet breath, he could hear the sound of silence breaking. The smell of hot tea wafted from a nearby window. He remembered that his old apartment, his fortress and domicile, was just around the corner.

The boy smelled the smoke of a wood kiln in the distance. The kiln burnt up the night, his chest, and his heart. His breath was cold, though the night was hot. The chirping of crickets brought no comfort. They all seemed to be yelling in unison, "Run, Run, RUN!!!" As the boy's feet began carrying him, he felt a pain in his gut that launched free his memories. He remembered his first loves, the first time he felt hate, and the inconsequentiality of those emotions. He remembered when he first thought…no, first learned that to really live, to really BE alive, you must learn to let go before you appreciate receiving. Love was not about owning, but about daily realization and sharing. It was about overcoming one's personal fiction, and learning to observe the ever-present new truths that emerged each day. The crickets yelled again.

Reaching his apartment, he quieted his mind and pressed his key into the lock. The lingering taste of the hot night invaded his mouth with each breath. He stiffened. The key turned. The lock clicked. The door opened. The boy entered his apartment. Immediately, he knew that the woman was gone, for she had never really been there at all. He realized in the quiet of the moment that the woman had been there to teach him a lesson, a reminder of his gained life experience. She, like other lonely ones, was only a child with an adult body. He dropped to the floor. He wept. He remembered. He looked up and saw a cold, wet closet with an open door containing a chair. He entered the closet and sat down. Then, he realized that the chair was not really there. It was a symbol, a manifestation of his mind's eye, a time machine, a translator of memories. He asked, "Am I the time machine?" He closed his eyes.

The time machine returned the boy to where he belonged, neither home nor in a strange land. He was in a place that encompasses a self-assured appreciation of just being. He began to recognize what trust appeared to be, what it tasted like, and how it felt in his mouth. He chewed; it was gritty, satisfying, and temporary, but it left an indelible aftertaste in his mouth. He cringed. He smiled. He laughed. He bit his lip. He opened his eyes. He was alive. Indeed, he had the collective experiences of everyone that had touched his heart. Each person had added to his time machine. He realized that, because of this, he was never truly alone. "Time to confront the past and reveal the present. Where shall I travel to next?"

II

The Open Field

The time machine whirred to a halt. When the boy opened his eyes, he was in the middle of an open field. All was quiet except for the whistle of the wind blowing through the old creaking trees. Each gust carried recollections of the past when children once played in that meadow. Echoes of laughter burst into the boy's memory. The sound of footsteps caused him to turn around, but all he saw was a faceless scarecrow. Strangely, the scarecrow reminded him of the lonely one, the personification of a child in an adult's body. The scarecrow looked longingly over the open field as if remembering times when people were there to watch over.

Suddenly, the voices of mothers and fathers called for their children to come home. The only things the boy heard in response were the fervent gusts of the wild wind carrying empty substance. But then, someone answered; it was a bull's cry.

The boy tripped, falling over. As he looked around, he saw the bull. It was old, gnarled, and barely able to stand, but still, its crystal white eyes pierced through the boy. He backpedaled, ramming his spine into a fence. He scrambled to his feet, grasped the fence, and crawled through the slats. However, all that waited for him on the other side was a cliff overlooking a deep ravine. The boy tried to gain his footing, but he slipped off the edge and tumbled down. Below him, the sound of crashing waves echoed in his ears. As he fell, he wept and then, pausing, felt at peace as a fog horn beckoned in the distance. He closed his eyes.

When the boy opened his eyes, he was at the bottom of the ravine. Nothing was around him but a desert, and some animals quietly surveying the area. Feeling the stern but gentle flow of the wind, he took a deep breath. Amidst the dry and muggy land, the smell of fresh water was near. He was by an oasis. As he caught sight of the watering hole, he walked over to it, bent down, cupped his hands, and drank deeply of the crisp liquid. It was sugar in his mouth, so sweet and satisfying. He smiled…he laughed. He brought more to his desperate lips, but it had turned to tea. Golden in color and even sweeter than the water, the tea reminded him of the warmth of his loved ones. The ones who were always and forever a part of him. He could feel each part of him being quenched and restored. He closed his eyes and took in the full aroma of the tea, and his surroundings.

When the boy opened his eyes, he was out of the ravine and back in the open field. He listened for the voices of the children and their parents, but they were silent. They were at peace. The sun began rising, revealing the beginnings of a new day. The boy gazed into the clearing and said, "Thank you."

The grass in the field, as if responding, brushed gently against the boy's skin, caressing his body. Though the boy heard no audible words, the grass seemed to be rustling the phrase, "Live." The boy smiled as he got to his feet. He closed his eyes, focused his mind, and entered the time machine.

III

The Falling Forest

As day broke, the sun shone in the boy's eyes, rousing him awake. After wiping the grogginess from his eyes, he realized he was falling through the sky! He was plummeting toward a forest full of dense evergreens. They were almost reaching toward him as if to catch him. He was thrust further into cognizance the longer he descended. He became filled not with fear, but rather a sense of realization that he had to act to save himself.

The evergreens caught him as he landed in their embrace.

The boy tasted iron in his mouth as the verdant branches broke his fall. Fragrant and frail jasmine flowers surrounded him, almost seeming to be speaking to him. Within the ethereal snowy petals of the jasmine flowers, he saw the face of someone he loved, someone he had not seen in what felt like ages. Their features were blurry, but he knew it was her. As he began to lose consciousness, he saw her smile back at him. Then, a huge weight began surrounding him, and he again slipped into unconsciousness.

————

The boy awoke to snowing. He took deep breaths; they went in like ice and came out like fire. A sense of longing entered his head, stretched through his body, and radiated outward, making him gasp. At first, he pushed the feeling away, but then he allowed it to return and envelop him. His eyes filled with tears as he felt the gentle embrace of the one he loved. As he accepted this feeling, the soft jasmine flowers around him all drooped for a moment, reflecting the mood that permeated the air. The boy closed his eyes. With intention this time, he took a warm breath inward. A small spark of life entered his chest and found its way into his heart. Slowly a fire kindled within him. He knew he needed to continue healing to understand how to let go of what was no longer needed.

The sky began to brighten, revealing a ray of warm summer light; the sun was responding to the boy. A smile found its way to his lips, and he found a tear at the edge of his eye. Without hesitation, the forest began transforming to reflect the arrival of spring. The boy thought he could hear a voice emanating from the woods in a child's timbre, yet also like the combined sounds of his loved ones. It reassured him by saying, "The night is done. The day is almost here."

Slowly, the boy began realizing that the voice was his own quiet reassurance resonating within his psyche—within his own heart.

Again, the voice said: "Live. Be fully and absolutely alive."

Without hesitation, the boy stood. When he looked straight ahead, he saw a very old bristlecone pine with a knothole in it. Inside the knothole, something shined so brightly that it blinded him. Cautiously, he approached the tree, and as he reached inside it, he felt something warm. He realized that the shining object was a key.

Brandishing the key, the boy studied his surroundings. He saw the closet with the chair inside a large knothole of another old bristlecone pine. Feeling excited, the boy entered the pine, walked into the closet, and sat in the chair. As the time machine rumbled to life, he prepared himself to unlock the next part of his journey.

IV
The Constantly Shifting Tide Of Perception

The sky was cloaked behind the soft shade of the boy's eyelids. The wind gently caressed his hair and lashes as he opened his eyes. Immediately, he was struck by how the sky changed from night to day within 10-second intervals. "What…why…when am I?". The forward momentum of time urged the boy to his feet. With some effort, he stood up, all the while feeling the pull of time propel him into consciousness.

All the shadows under the trees mirrored this oddity by continuously signaling the arrival of morning and departure of night. As his vision cleared, the boy noticed that in the daylight, he saw the vestiges of people flashing between the trees. Some of them he had never seen—or at least that he had never consciously discerned—before. The boy stepped further into the moving shadows and noticed projections painting the trees. They were reflections of entire scenes unfolding before him. With realization in his heart, the boy said, "These...these are people from memories...my life...my own memories." Each of these memories collided with one another. Time began to flatten into a single plane, and any perception of timelines became an illusion.

Confronted with so many people and events from his life, the boy felt like a stranger in the homeland of his own mind. He knew each event intimately, but there were subtle details that he had either forgotten, or had attempted to erase. He began noticing facets he had not perceived before. Being a stranger in a familiar land allowed him to explore his mind with new eyes, finding home within the unknown sections of his past.

Suddenly, the boy heard the sound of the lonely one behind him. She was the woman his mind conjured when the time machine returned him to Kentucky. Her voice was soft yet stern, a summer night shifting to a bitter and biting cold. There was longing in her tone that brought a tear to the boy's eye.

She said, "I remember you. I remember your face. Do you remember mine?"

He said, "Yes, I remember. You float through my summer nights like a refreshing breeze, always returning and reminding me that there is more of life to be discovered." He laughed, and shed another tear.

"Yes, oh yes, dear friend. We are the same, you and I," she said.

He questioned her further. "Who are you?".

She said, "You have known of me, dear old friend, for without you, I cannot be whole."

"Why do you torture me?!"

She gently touched the boy's chin. After kneeling down and pulling his face to her level, she stared deeply into his eyes and said, "Because...I am not charged with doing that. No one but you can allow such a thing to happen."

As more tears fell, he closed his eyes, and turned away before remarking, "But why are you here?"

She paused and exhaled a gentle laugh, replying, "Because...you talk the way that people laugh."

Warmth welled up inside him, and the boy began to cry hot tears of happiness. He was loved, and he was alive. He could not forget that. When he opened his eyes, the woman was gone. His heart-beat was whole and soft. It felt like summer in his chest, like gentle rain joining the rivers that eventually meet the ocean. He didn't need to wonder why she was no longer there because she never left him. She was his heart, always beating to remind him that he was never alone.

He remembered. He slowed his breath and felt the wind surround him. He felt the time machine calling to him. He gazed over to the horizon, and the chair of the time machine was waiting for him. This time, the chair was not inside of a tree or darkened by shadow but truly bathed in light. It reflected the morning sun more brilliantly than he had ever seen before. He smiled and made his way to the chair. Taking a seat, the boy breathed the last vestiges of summer warmth. He closed his eyes and the time machine sent him on his next journey.

Part 2

The Traveler and The Boy

V

Dreaming Ourselves to Survival

A phone rang. "Who could be calling the time machine at this hour?" The traveler thought as he walked over to pick it up. But the receiver passed right through his hand when he tried touching it. The traveler put intention and heart into grasping the phone, and that time he succeeded.

"Hello," he asked.

"Hello Mijo, it's your grandpa."

The traveler's heart dropped for a moment. His grandfather had passed away over ten years ago. How was this possible?

"Grandpa?"

"Mijo, where did you put the corn flakes? I can't find them anywhere. You know I have to have my corn flakes in the morning."

On the other end of the line, the traveler heard a

boy's voice; his voice as a child answered back to his grandfather, saying, "It's on top of the refrigerator, Grandpa! Remember?"

His grandfather responded warmly, separated by the mist of decades. "Yes Mijo, I remember now. How could I forget?"

The traveler spoke into the past, "I love you, Grandpa. I will always love you."

His grandfather paused for a second, and then said, "Mijo, is that you? You got so big, I can tell."

The traveler smiled and responded, "We have so much to talk about."

"I know you already know I love you too, Mijo." The sound of rain invaded the line. It grew louder and louder until his grandfather's voice was pushing through a thick mist of time. Still, the traveler heard his grandfather's last words. "I love you, Mijo."

Like a fossilized memory, the traveler felt an ancient evergreen in the forest of his heart take root once again. "I love you too, but I can never go back," the traveler said.

Suddenly, the boy who had been with his grandfather was next to the traveler. He was startled for a moment when the boy touched his hand. The boy was the traveler as a child, and his child-self was staring up at him.

"It's okay. You don't have to be afraid anymore," the boy said. Stepping closer, he added, "Together, we can find the question. We were never far apart to begin with. So, shall we go?"

The traveler froze for a moment, then said, "Yes, but where are we going?"

"Can't you see, we are already here."

———

They were in a vast room with a door at the end of it.

"Where are we?" The traveler asked the boy.

The boy handed him a key and said, "Why don't you find out."

"Sure."

The traveler walked to the door and put the key in the lock, but it did not fit.

"What's wrong?"

"It doesn't fit. The key doesn't fit the lock." The Traveler realized that the key didn't fit the lock because…"I don't belong here."

"Why not?"

"Because," the traveler took a breath, "I am not that person anymore. Yet, I will always be," his eye bore into the boy's, "you."

The boy reached into his pocket and found another key. The traveler noticed the lock was very long and narrow. Then, the traveler tried both keys simultaneously, and the door unlocked.

Before the traveler could see what was inside, the boy jumped in front of him. He began opening the door but stopped just before the traveler could see passed it.

The boy asked, "Are you ready?"

The traveler nodded, and together, they walked inside.

VI

The Confluence Of Blue Thread

The traveler and the boy had entered a large warehouse full of tangled red thread. The space was heavy with the feeling of angst. Touching each line sparked different memories the traveler did not know he recalled. As the traveler traversed the tangle of red thread, he noticed the boy was no longer by his side. Panic pulsed through his veins. He scoured for him, his eyes landing on an especially tight tangle of red amassed at a singular spot. The boy had become tangled in the fibers, allowing the overwhelming sense of angst within the space to engulf him. The traveler ran toward the boy but stopped when he heard someone call out.

"Who are you?" a voice asked.

The traveler froze when he realized the voice was all around him. The red thread was communicating.

Still unsure, he calmly responded, "I am a traveler. I found this place with the help of the boy."

The red fibers abruptly stated, "I see the boy in your eyes. You are one and the same." The traveler stared at the crimson thread with a perplexed and partially surprised expression. His vision blurred. He gazed down, and three scarlet chords had tangled around his wrist. "You lie to yourself," the thread harshly revealed; next posing, "Why are you here, and who are you really?"

"I am," the word almost got stuck in the traveler's throat, but he was able to push it out, "alive."

The threads loosened, and the space felt slightly less heavy.

"Yes, my friend," the scarlet chords responded. "You have passed through many time periods and many peoples' lives, yet you never realized the truth. The truth about," the red thread grew loud, filling the entire warehouse as it said, "the time machine."

"I know that the time machine is the collected knowledge of my loved ones. The ones who fill my heart and make me whole."

The three strands that encircled the traveler's wrist said, "No. No, it is much more than that. Ask the boy if you must Traveler."

Tears began brimming in his eyes as he gazed at the boy. The traveler grasped the boy's hand.

"You already know, my friend," the boy said.

The traveler's lips grew into a gentle smile as he

replied, "The time machine is the confluence of collected memories. It is the hurt, love, and lessons learned. The time machine is one's ability to access the past through memory to find peace in the present. People and their love are the moving parts."

As if satisfied with this answer, the crimson thread began dissipating and released the boy, who landed in the traveler's arms. The feeling of warm summer wind filled the traveler's chest, and the fibers fell away from his wrist. However, one thread remained—it was blue. This sapphire strand ran to the other end of the warehouse and through a cracked door.

The boy, already at the door, asked the traveler, "Are you ready to embark on the next step of our journey?"

"Yes. I'm ready now. Show me."

The blue thread loosened, and the traveler continued through the door with the boy.

$$VII$$

The Train of Seasons

Even with eyes closed, the feeling of the wind was soft and warm as tropical dew. Immediately, the traveler felt reborn, restored. The difficulties he had traversed and the people he had met, those experiences sat softly and confidently in his heart. The traveler could find home wherever he went, any time or place. Nothing was impossible, and everything could be accessed to provide knowledge to facilitate new growth of mind and heart.

It was a good thing the traveler felt that realization because when he opened his eyes, what he saw caused him to hesitate in his strides. The sky was Prussian blue and deep navy with highlights of cadmium yellow. Light flashed in and out of focus within the room...no, within the car he was now in.

The sound of a soft atmospheric whistle filled the space. It was so gentle that it blended seamlessly with the night yet simultaneously split the air like internalized screams of a lonely heart. He gathered he was on a train heading somewhere. Looking down, he noticed the boy sleeping; his head rested on the traveler's shoulder.

Sunset was upon them both. He felt as though he had slept for weeks, yet the exhaustion of a long and tenuous journey weighed on his limbs. The traveler gently lifted the boy's head, setting it on the cushion adjacent to their seat. The traveler stood and ventured outside of the train car.

As the traveler exited the car, he entered the train's main hallway. Feeling something on his wrist, he gazed down and was greeted by a small strand of blue thread wrapped around it. The line was fragile and bright like fireflies on a warm summer night. The fibers began to glow as he touched it, setting the traveler's mind at rest. Remembering what the scarlet chord had told him, he continued onward, closing the train car door behind him.

As the traveler looked out the window, the horizon revealed no familiar landmarks. All was new and unknown. At the opposite end of the hallway, someone hastily exited their train car while clearing their throat. The traveler was astonished when he took in the passenger's face and hands—indeed, the parts of their body not covered by clothing—were completely transparent! The partially invisible passenger reached into their pocket and pulled out a train ticket. With that, a bell clanged, and a loud and forceful voice came over the train's intercom: "Tickets, please! Everyone present your tickets for the conductor to collect!"

The traveler reached into his pocket without delay and found two crumpled pieces of paper. But upon pulling the pieces from his pocket, he noticed they were also completely transparent! The traveler took care not to drop them as footsteps came from just outside the car's hallway entrance. The faceless, see-through form of the conductor walked into the hallway and began collecting tickets from each passenger, all of whom were in various levels of opacity.

Examining his hand, the traveler realized he was becoming translucent himself! Though, he was not as diaphanous as the other passengers.

The conductor approached him. He aimed his invisible gaze at the traveler and asked, "Are your tickets on hand?"

The traveler responded, "Yes, here they are."

Without another word, the conductor collected the sheer tickets. He stamped them, making the paper materialize just before they were pocketed.

The traveler began to wonder where the train was taking them all. Scanning the destination cards on the train, he found the word "Home" inscribed on placards. Curiosity washed over the traveler, and to his surprise and delight, a grin slowly emerged on his face. The traveler took a moment to walk to one of the train car windows and watched as the sun set.

Time seemed endless there as everything passed by deliberately yet thoughtfully. Once in a while, the train would reach a stop, and passengers would get off. However, there were never any visible land masses to speak of at these stops, only an endless ocean as far as the eye could see. Also, each passenger would not walk straight into the sunset but down pathways that led underneath the vast ocean. As time passed, the traveler noticed no one ever boarded the train, only exited it.

Once, the traveler called out to a passenger departing, saying, "Farewell! Enjoy your journey."

However, the passenger would only turn their head, and a smile materialized on their semi to fully transparent faces as they faded. They would then disappear into the seemingly cavernous pathways that led under the endless ocean stretching beyond the train stops.

The smell of a new summer, temperate and unknown, swept across the traveler's gossamer face as the sun began to rise. His body grew warm as he took in a breath full of intention. He smiled and then, feeling contented, returned to the train car where the boy was enjoying his breakfast.

"Did you sleep well?" asked the traveler.

"Very, thank you," replied the boy. "Where are we going?"

"We will find out soon enough."

"Wherever it is, I am sure we will face it together, my friend."

The boy finished his breakfast, and they both settled in, preparing for their destination.

VIII
Breath: The Vessel of Intention

Suddenly, there was cheering in the background. The boy was roused from his slumber and felt a cold shiver down his spine. The sound of joy emanating from outside the train car brought little comfort for some reason. Curious, the boy left the sleeping traveler in the train car to investigate. The boy noticed something outside their room, a clear balloon with a slowly dwindling flame inside. A thin piece of white string attached the balloon to their doorknob. It bobbed silently in the air, and seemed to move in erratic patterns.

When the boy touched the balloon, his hand felt as cold as a January night in the dead of winter! He pulled his hand away and watched as the balloon's flame began to fluctuate. As the boy breathed into his hands to warm them, he saw it flare as it grew slightly in intensity. In fact, every time he breathed, the fire would respond.

The boy exhaled heavily onto the balloon, and it blazed exponentially! Startled, the boy drew back, only to see the fire shrink into a flickering spark.

"What are you?" the boy questioned.

Though he was unsure, the boy tied the balloon to his wrist, deciding to bring it along. He then focused his attention on investigating the source of the cheering. Upon exiting the door leading to the dining area, the boy noticed a group of passengers cheering intermittently at the far end of the train car. The boy spotted a series of flashes emanating from a window near the commotion. He stuck his head out of the window and what the boy saw astonished him. There were hundreds of balloons with burning flames inside departing the train!

He decided to inspect things closer, so he ran through the large group of passengers, making his way to the front. When he reached the door, he noticed that one of the passengers was breathing very thoughtfully and in an extremely focused manner. He remarked that each of these passengers were holding a clear balloon with a flame dancing inside each one. The passenger breathing thoughtfully seemed to fade away and reappear with their breaths; each inhale made the passenger visible, and each exhale made them translucent.

Almost without warning, the passenger turned his gaze toward the group, and began smiling at everyone. Then, everyone began cheering as the passenger took one deep inhale, and then out, vanishing from sight! With that, the balloon that the passenger was holding flew off into the sky and over the horizon, joining with the hundreds of others.

One of the passengers turned to the boy and asked him, "Have you set your intentions yet?"

"Excuse me, what?" the boy inquired.

"Your breath, have you aligned your breath to your intentions?"

The boy stated, "I'm not sure."

"Ah, you have time, but it is never too late to begin doing so, Friend."

The boy suddenly felt warmth rise up from within his chest, then his throat, and then fill his mouth. A long warm exhale filled the air around him, and his balloon's flame grew. He thought of his loved ones, his life back home, and how far he had traveled. It filled him with purpose, joy, and a bit of sadness. "I'm never alone. As long as I have love, I will find the trust and hope to continue."

The passenger smiled tenderly as the boy gently laughed with joy.

"You are ready," stated the passenger.

"Ready for what?"

"To continue on your journey."

"But," the boy gasped for words, "I have a friend

on board that I need to see first."

"My young friend, he knows where to find you. You will not ever be far off. Your paths will cross again."

As heat filled his body, a smile rose to the boy's lips before he said, "Goodbye. Thank you." Then the boy turned translucent and faded transparent before disappearing completely from sight. As he did, the balloon's flame burned bright. It floated up into the night sky, and over the horizon just as the sun began to rise.

A moment later, the sound of cheering gently roused the traveler. Feeling comfortable and relaxed, he smiled and fell back to sleep. The faint sound of cheering was drowned out by metal wheels against tracks and howling whistles calling out to the early morning. In his last moments before slipping back into slumber, the traveler felt the words, *thank you,* reach his heart.

IX
Veiled Behind Serene Eyes

The traveler opened his eyes and realized that he was no longer on the train; he was in a forest. However, he was alone. The boy was nowhere to be found.

Suddenly, the ground thrummed with the cry of a wolf breaking through the silence. With each passing moment, he could hear the wolf's howls and snarls of anger as it came closer...and closer. The traveler was being hunted.

The traveler began to run, unsure of where to find safety. He darted around but lost his footing, falling off a cliff's edge. Tumbling down into a ravine, the traveler hobbled until he reached a corner. After scanning his surroundings, he realized that there was no way out.

"Alright! If you seek me, here I am," cried the traveler.

The shadow of the wolf hovered over the cliff-face, eclipsing the traveler. The beast gave one last howl, and the traveler heard the desperation in it's timbre.

"I'm ready," cried the traveler.

The wolf snarled as it descended the cliff-side, stopping only a few yards away from the traveler. The creature locked eyes with him.

With one final breath, the traveler roared, "I'm not afraid! Come at me!"

With intense speed, the beast lunged at the traveler. Suddenly, the traveler's fists dropped in remorse. Without knowing why, the traveler opened his arms to the wolf. In the moments that followed, the anger shattered as the wolf froze a few inches from the traveler. Then, it gently pressed its head against him, and the traveler tenderly hugged the wolf in return. An instant later, the wolf shed its grizzly fur to reveal the gaze of a friend – the boy.

At first, the traveler felt the drenching downpour of a thousand rainfalls. The ground felt wet with rain. However, in reality, it was two drops of wetness, two tears that filled the corners of his eyes. The quiet trembling of his breath released a torrent of emotions; ones once trapped behind the forest of his mind that a dam stood watch over to ensure his heart wouldn't drown. He looked down at the boy—his child self—

and the boy's eyes filled his gaze with the force of an earthquake only they could feel.

"Say it," the boy pushed out, "and this time, really mean it. Why am I really here?"

"What is in my heart, in your heart. All the broken parts, the hidden sadness and anger is killing us." The traveler pleaded with the boy. "For me to let that pain go, you must let go of it too."

"I can't," whimpered the boy.

"It's time to let go. This time, say it," the traveler's next words came out firm but full of tenderness as he added, "and really mean it."

The traveler looked around the forest; it was scorched and burned. However, upon noticing the charred earth surrounding him, he perceived that the soil had new growth, and was giving forth life. He took a breath, realizing some forests only grow after old and dead matter is cleared away. The traveler felt his heart growing like a tree within him. The earth, green with life, seemed to solder together all that was living. The traveler knew that new growth could arise even through loss. All must move forward, and everything flowers with each emerging season. He thrived, understanding his heart could open and close with every passing season. Wiping tears from his eyes, he fully embraced the boy and felt whole again.

"I forgive you," said the boy.

The traveler responded, "I forgive you."

The wind sang slow and steady as he raised his eyes to a nearby tree. It was suddenly, bathed in richly verdant greenery and the warmest autumn light. Inside the nearby tree was a chair. The time machine called to the boy, and the traveler knew as soon as the boy smiled at him. Without hesitancy, the traveler let the boy go, knowing the boy had found peace. As the boy neared the tree and sat in the chair, the forest began to let forth blooms.

With his final words, "thank you," the boy was returned home.

The traveler knew the boy was never gone from his heart. The traveler realized that one must look past adversities and challenges that seem like a fierce wolf because they are something vulnerable within ourselves. They need understanding, for they are both beautiful and heart-wrenchingly sad, smiling inside us like a mouth full of broken china. One cannot forever hide the quiet madness, veiled behind serene eyes dew-wetted by the realization of life.

Part 3

The Traveler

X

The Realization of Forgiveness Found

The traveler walked down an empty road, full of nothing in particulars whispering in his ears on the wind. The road seemed endless, with no buildings or signs to speak of. Yet, the traveler knew all roads must lead to an end at some point. The path seemed to be winding more and more as he traversed it. It felt as though it was searching for an end just as much as he was.

After passing a clearing of verdant green trees, the traveler saw a crossroads come into focus. The paths were identical, and the smell in the air hinted that there was new growth in bloom on both. However, upon closing his eyes and focusing his senses, the traveler pressed one foot on each road. He noticed the earth was fresh, wild, and unpaved on one road, while the other was fully paved, structured, and familiar. Both felt like routes home. One smelled of verdant greenery and trust. The second wafted of overripe fruits in the summer, comfortable and known.

Upon opening his eyes, love beat steadily in the traveler's heart. A pang of loss began to ache, but then subside. When he faced this choice previously, being reborn and facing the unknown, he chose to leave all he knew to be fully realized. Even so, this proved to be, in many ways, an escape. However, he knew he had to return to what was known and use the lessons he learned to face who he had become. He chose to go down the paved road filled with the scent of overripe fruits on each tree. It was time to gain a new appreciation for what he had not allowed himself to see before.

The wind smelled of confluence, a joining of mind and heart filled with intention. Yet, every few yards, he would notice the stumps of dead trees appearing, and ache a bit inside. Birds sang a song in nearby trees. However, their tone almost sounded alarmed like a warning. Was it a warning for their kin or the traveler? He continued walking. The traveler spotted a decaying bird on the roadside. Though he only saw it for an instant, the quiet mood of that moment gave him pause. Without realizing it, there was a change in the texture of the road beneath him; with his next step he had found his way onto an old wooden bridge.

The smell of a mossy waterway drifted into his

nostrils. The wind caressed his face, and he felt at peace, then in love, and next he felt affirmed within himself. A voice reached out, and his ears perked up. They twitched when he heard the words, "Are you looking for someone?" Gazing slowly behind him, and then downward, the traveler saw a girl around 12 years old.

He responded, "Oh, I thought I was alone on this bridge. Hello."

She smirked and gave a little laugh, saying, "We are seldom alone, but when we are, isn't it when we feel most alive?"

The traveler chuckled to himself, thinking that was an intriguing thing to say. "I suppose that is when you can focus without the noise of everything else in your ear."

Her lips stretched from ear to ear, making dimples appear on both cheeks.

"Can we walk together?"

He pondered, and then responded, "Sure, I don't see why not."

It was nice to have a friend on this road. Maybe he had chosen a meaningful path by taking the one he had previously decided to avoid.

Suddenly, a car appeared over the horizon and passed them both. As the car disappeared from sight, the girl pointed straight ahead and told the traveler,

"Look! There's my friend! I'll introduce you both."

The traveler beamed at her enthusiasm, saying, "Okay."

When the girl's friend came into view, and her face into better focus, he realized that he recognized her. His eyes widened as he saw that the girl's friend was a woman. She was someone both young and old, a woman whose face continually seemed to change. He saw warmth in her eyes and expressions; the kindness of his family and friends were in her smile. As she came into yet clearer view, she extended her hand to shake his, and he finally *saw* her.

She spoke to the traveler saying, "Hello there. I see that you met my young friend."

The traveler had never met her before, yet there was something familiar that he couldn't quite understand. He extended his hand to shake her's. When they touched her warmth felt like the summers of his childhood. She had a gentle face with eyes that were like a campfire. Her grin was a duality of elements, sustained warmth, yet quietly overpowering in the way an uncontrolled fire could level a forest. His heart felt full, and his mind was betwixt it all. He regained his senses in what was merely an instant but felt like unending time.

He responded, "Hello. Yes, we met on the road. You both look alike. Are you related?"

She only smiled briefly and said, "We are peas in a pod, us two." The girl grasped the woman's hand with delight. She then asked, "Won't you join us? We are on our way home, and you look like you could use a meal and a place to rest."

He noticed it was getting dark, so he smiled and nodded in acceptance.

They talked about many things on the walk home. They laughed, and shared stories of life and all things pleasant yet heartbreakingly human. The traveler felt at home with them. Finally, they reached a cabin next to the largest and most verdant trees that he had ever seen.

The woman then told him, "This is home for now. We have to run, but we will see you again."

He grinned and felt a warm breeze with the promise of several everlasting summers fill his hair. The scent lingered there as if it made its home within him.

He responded, "Yes, I'll look forward to it. Goodnight."

They waved goodbye to him and continued down the road. Turning away for a moment, he heard the girl's laughter as she bid him goodbye. Upon turning around, he saw that they were gone. Rather than worry, he felt at ease with himself, knowing he would see them again.

The traveler walked into the cabin and felt the light paint his face in a heavy coat of ordinary. He enjoyed the sensation, smiling and chuckling to himself. His body relaxed for the first time in years, it seemed. He realized that he was calm. He gazed at a nearby window where a table rested. On the table, there was a teapot and a few cups. Close by there was a stovetop and kettle for making tea. He beamed as he reached into his pocket. There, he found his favorite tea that he had been saving. He filled the kettle with water from a sink, boiled it, and sat in the chair.

He felt a transitory serenity, but it still felt like freedom. Indeed, for he was free and full of thankfulness. The traveler realized that if one allowed it, they would arrive at the heart's doorstep. He felt at peace with his identity as a traveler, friend, and family to many. He had now found a place to rest. He brewed his first cup of tea, sipped it, and knew he was ready for the morning. After all, how we respond to our feelings was the greatest freedom. The feelings we invest in are where we invest our life.

XI
The Silk Ladder

At first, only the sound of the traveler's breath was gently resting on the air. A quiet but tired feeling made its way through the cabin as the sunrise worked its way over the mountainside. A small beam of light rested heavily on the traveler's closed lids, which caused his eyes to open softly. The bright ray was overpowering at first but quickly gave way to a gentle and pleasant warmth. Turning his head toward the brilliance, the traveler watched the sun finish its lethargic ascent over the horizon. "Heh, well, good morning to you too, Sky. You look about as tired as I do," mused the traveler.

Just as quickly as the blue sky radiated warmth, a slow collection of gray clouds crept in. They made their presence known with cracks of thunder, quiet at first and then booming. The sky turned a hazy blue-green. "Hmmm, storm's coming. So much for that sunny day I was hoping for." Outside, the branches of nearby trees began whipping, becoming louder until they almost seemed to be singing a panicked lament. Only then did the traveler hear the sounds of the erupting sky accompanied by a large branch cracking open and hitting the ground.

With a start, the traveler rushed to the window to survey the storm's size. As he began to open it, scents of ozone, petrichor, and mineral-rich water wafted in. "That's not just a storm." The wind roared and seemed to be approaching the cabin. The traveler quickly dressed and stepped outside to survey the full damage caused by this happening. As the traveler looked behind the cabin, his eyes widened in partial horror, amazement, and realization. A hurricane was forming in the sky just over the horizon. "No...but it's coming too fast. I won't be able to outrun it." The traveler scanned his surroundings for a car, a bicycle, or even people, but he was alone. "What now?" the traveler inquired. He searched for a cellar but found none. Noticing the hurricane was rapidly approaching, he ran back inside. He snatched a thick blanket, heading for the bathroom; covering himself, he took refuge inside the bathtub. "It's not much, but it will do."

The traveler heard the hurricane, which sounded like a crashing waterfall colliding with a freight train. The strong scent of fresh cut grass cut deeply into his memories. He felt the first shaking of the house's structure, signaling that it was beginning to be pulled apart. The ceiling fractured, and the windows shattered as they were ripped apart. The roof flew off as the hurricane passed. The traveler's body went limp as he was lifted out of the cabin and torn from the bathtub. The traveler's memories erupted, hearing the soft sounds of a piano before losing consciousness as he was sucked into the eye of the storm.

———

The traveler woke up realizing he was in a completely peaceful and calm place; the hurricane sounded distant and almost quiet. Startled by the sudden tranquility, he moved his arm only to find that he was tangled up in some material and suspended in the air. "It's soft yet sturdy," he said. As the traveler's vision cleared, he noticed that he was entwined in a collection of delicate yet surprisingly strong threads. He was tethered to a structure consisting of rungs made of silk. "It's...it's a silk ladder." Grasping the fabric, the traveler felt the silk rungs beginning to release their grip on him. He panicked for a moment and felt his heart jump but then noticed that the silk ladder embraced him again once he loosened his hold. As the traveler gazed up, softening his grip, the ladder began lifting him to the top of the hurricane. Pulled far above, the traveler saw only open blue sky. He allowed himself, and yes, willed himself calm and responsive as he made his way up the silk ladder.

He noticed that above him, a figure was climbing down to meet him. It...it was the woman he met on the road the previous day. She slowly and carefully descended, letting the silk ladder bring her to the traveler's eye level.

"Hello," she said.

"Hi," said the traveler.

"Well, what a circumstance this is, isn't it? Do you know how to make it to the top?" she asked the traveler.

"No, I suppose I just want to find some solid ground."

"Many people have been where you are now," she took a breath before continuing, "Indeed, I am one of them. However, what most of them, most of us, need to develop is the resilience of perspective."

"What...?" he asked.

"This storm...this hurricane...will pass, but you need to listen; all of us do well to listen when faced with unknown situations. We often forget that all things pass by and that nothing persists indefinitely. Why do you think we learn best from what tears us down? It helps us to find perspective, to appreciate that all things pass and that we are much stronger than the situations that press us in."

Realizing that he was just about near the top of the hurricane, the traveler looked around and saw the biggest and clearest blue sky he had ever seen. He felt dwarfed by its expansiveness. It was terrifyingly beautiful.

As they both rested on the top rung, the woman stated, "Once you learn to sit with fear, you begin learning how to love without being dominated by it. We often must become familiar with letting go before we learn to appreciate getting anything."

The traveler responded by saying, "It's so beautiful up here. Where do we go from here?"

She answered, "We can't ever know exactly, but I have a feeling that we will see you again soon."

"We?" the traveler asked.

Looking down the rungs, the traveler saw the girl from the road suspended in the silk. She smiled at him, gave a small laugh, and waved hello. With that, the traveler grew tired and slowly drifted into a quiet slumber.

As the traveler opened his eyes, he found himself in a bed. He reached down and felt a rung from the silk ladder extending from his pocket. He then pushed the rest of the silk into his pocket, stood up, and walked to a nearby window. What he saw left him speechless. He was in a vast, glistening city with hundreds of doors on each building. There was no end to the doors. The air felt cool and soft, reminding him of his childhood home. He thought he smelled something familiar—his grandmother's cooking.

As he turned around and saw the exit, the smell became stronger. Finally, he walked to the door, turned the knob, and opened it. With tears welling in his eyes, he noticed the figures of his grandparents making breakfast. "My family...here?" he inquired.

Walking up to them, he noticed that they didn't acknowledge him. He tried to touch them, but he heard a familiar voice call his name before he could. It was the girl that he met on the road. She had entered through a door at the opposite end.

She said, "Hello again. Do you know where you are?"

"No, but it's wonderful! Where am I?" he asked.

She responded by saying, "This is the City of Memories. You have much to learn about this place. Many people are waiting to see you."

Then slowly, she extended her hand to him. After he grasped it, they both walked through a door leading to the city streets.

XII

The City of Memories

"What is this place?" asked the traveler of the girl.

She responded, "A very old place, one you likely haven't heard of. Many people have been through here but never slowed down enough to realize they were here."

The Traveler looked at the girl with a perplexed expression. She smiled a bit and giggled but noticed he needed some clarity.

She straightened her expression and, in a more serious tone, stated, "You are here because you are at a crossroads. We have many realizations in our lives. However, when we take the time to examine our choices and know that we can do better, we can then look inward and find this place."

The traveler observed that each street was

surrounded by large dark blue and light purple buildings, each with its own unique door. Some buildings were three to four stories tall. The sky was a beautiful collection of sunset oranges and reds, and the streets were tranquil. It wasn't until the traveler listened carefully to the ambient sounds that he noticed there were noises emanating from behind each door. Each building had several doors, and all were quietly alive with resonance. The more the traveler listened, the more he heard the sounds becoming apparent. In fact, the longer he listened to each, the more he began to recognize them. They were from memories—his memories. However, he didn't recognize all of them.

The girl smiled as she saw realization fill the empty spaces in his eyes. It was as though a nebula, a small universe, or a galaxy began populating his mind. The same vastness was in her eyes as well. "I am going to leave you to your explorations now, Friend," stated the girl.

"But which door, or doors, should I go through?" asked the traveler.

"There are thousands of doors, yes, many options. But you have probably already realized that each door contains deeply personal memories. However, many of these memories are from experiences buried deep within you that rest within the unconscious meanderings of your mind. So please, whichever door you enter, be attentive if someone responds when you interact with them. It is vital you observe and learn, for these memories likely have much to share with you."

The traveler, taking all of this in, stopped and pondered on these statements. He then asked, "Can I use my time machine? Is each door a time machine?"

"Your time machine was merely a collapsing and expanding of your perception as you delved into your conscious memories alone. However, these doors are the collective memories you have either forgotten or are no longer fully connected to. They are speaking in conference with you so that you can reconnect with them. So, in a sense, yes, they are."

The traveler asked one more question of the girl, "What if, when I am exploring, I meet someone that wants to come back with me to the City of Memories?"

The girl's eyes sparkled as she said, "Then be a welcoming host, and see to it that they feel welcome in the city. Maybe they will gravitate to you because they have something to teach you."

"What an amazing place. Where should I start?"

As the traveler looked around the city, he saw thousands of buildings and innumerable doors. When he did not hear the girl respond, he noticed that she was no longer by his side but by one of the doors. As she opened it, she became very serious, simply stating, "Just listen, and you will know what is best, Friend." Finally, the girl stepped through the threshold and closed it behind her.

The traveler began pondering which door he

should enter. But then, the traveler heard a familiar voice emanate from within him. It was faint, but he eventually heard a misty voice state, "Fear can lead to the emergence of the unknown. Still, fear is the catalyst for growth." The traveler recognized this voice.

"I remember you." The traveler touched his chest. "You have never been far from me. How are you, old friend?"

Within his mind's eye, he saw a woman, ethereal in her appearance. She had a soft but fervent tone, and the traveler remembered he was never alone. He remembered what the boy had taught him. "Oh hello, my dear friend," the familiar voice stated.

The traveler then said, "You are…."

"Yes, we are the same, you and I. Always connected. As one." The woman was his heart and the collective love of the cherished people in his life.

"It has been a long time since we've talked, hasn't it?" he asked her.

"For you, maybe. For me though, I speak with you often. Now, you are finally hearing me," stated his heart, and the traveler *was* listening.

After walking past several doors, a fervent voice spoke loudly in his ear and heart. He stopped, reached for the doorknob, turned it, and stepped inside.

XIII
Lessons From Waves

The traveler found himself inside an empty cottage, startling him so much he couldn't keep it from infecting his face. The cottage was ancient and smelled of dry oak and cedar. The floorboards creaked with each step he took inside. Small clouds of dust rose from the floorboards. Each scent carried remnants of memories that would rise and fall with passionate and fervent whispers in the traveler's heart.

As the reminisces became more intense, his heart was both warmed and chilled. "Why do I feel that I know this place? Where am I?" he remarked. The traveler looked out the window and what he saw caused his throat to tighten. A vast ocean was just outside, and the water level was steadily rising. In the distance, a giant cloud was heading toward him. "Fog?" Howling reverberated in the air as he saw what was approaching him. "No...," he remarked, realizing a giant wave was filling the horizon.

Feeling his feet carry him, he ran for the door to escape the cottage. The traveler's heart filled with growing dismay. As he turned the ancient copper doorknob, it didn't budge; the door was locked. The traveler heard the lapping of waves behind him just before the wetness encircled his ankles. He turned around and saw the water level slowly rising and moving throughout the cottage like a lonely bird attempting to escape a cage. As panic threatened to consume him, the traveler slowed his breathing. He remembered what the girl had told him; not all experiences or people within the rooms are memories but may be unresolved emotions seeking confluence within heart and mind. The traveler then realized that this cottage, this giant wave, and this place were all unconscious recollections of emotions from his past.

Suddenly, the traveler heard a click from the lock on the cottage door. With some effort, he turned the handle, and with a singular and fervent grunt, he pushed it, and the door opened. He spilled out with the water and was carried onto a rocky path. Pressing his hands against the ground, he was able to rise to his feet. The smell of petrichor filled the traveler's senses. As he steadied himself, he saw a long, thin pathway stretching ahead. Slowly, the traveler aimed his gaze at the horizon, seeing the giant wave getting closer. It was going to be upon him in a matter of minutes. With each step, portions of the pathway began to break apart. He had to traverse every step carefully. Then with one deep breath, the traveler bolted for the other side of the road.

When the traveler was halfway across, crashing waves ricocheted in his ears, and the ground beneath him began to degrade more quickly. The waters were swiftly tearing up the trail. Then, with sudden speed and accuracy, a massive wave plummeted onto a section of the road just ahead of him. Almost too swiftly, the wave engulfed the traveler, sweeping him into the vast ocean. All at once, the traveler felt his consciousness swallowed up by the heaviness of the wave. Then, feeling darkness encroach on him, his body let go as he fell unconscious.

The traveler was thrust into consciousness, forcefully unstitching his eyelids. As his vision cleared, he noticed that everything was hazy and dark. His body floated weightlessly as the weight of the water shifted his limbs back and forth. Unable to see his hand in front of his face, the traveler turned his gaze upward, observing a warm light shining far above him. He then realized he couldn't breathe, the weight of the water pushed brutally against his chest. When the traveler came to full consciousness, he found himself deep underwater. The instinct to survive pumped blood wildly from his rapidly beating heart. He forced himself upward, and after several excruciatingly eternal moments that defied time, the traveler broke through the surface. Simultaneously, he coughed up water and drew in a nourishing breath. He felt enlivening air fill his lungs, energizing and burning his insides. The waves tossed him back and forth. Becoming tired, the traveler let go and let himself float on his back. Slowly, the waters became less fervent.

The momentary break in the shifting current provided a reprieve; he surveyed his surroundings and noticed he was being carried back to shore. Grabbing a nearby crag, the traveler pressed himself against it, feeling the cold wetness of the rock against his face. As a laugh rose from his chest, the traveler saw the end of the narrow pathway was just ahead of him. Letting this expulsion, this release of emotions wash over him, he felt the waves carry him. Feeling both exhausted and relaxed, the traveler pulled himself onto dry land. Laying on his back, he rested and took time to fill his lungs with air. Turning his head, he noticed the sky was clear. However, when he squinted, there was a dark cloud over the horizon where another set of waves was building. Yet, with a grin, the traveler did not let this realization fill his heart with foreboding, for he knew he could withstand it.

With some effort, the traveler pulled himself onto his feet. Looking ahead on the path, he saw a large shallow cave. Inside the cave, he smelled the familiar scent of petrichor. After his eyes adjusted to the ambient darkness, sunlight broke through a hole in the top of the cave, and slowly he noticed a door made of rock at the far end. The traveler made his way to the door. Pressing his hand against the hinges of the rock door, he felt a warm breeze move across his fingertips. Lightly grasping the rocky handle, he cracked the door ever so slightly. Taking a peek inside, he noticed the City of Memories was on the other end. As he pulled the door open, he stopped, reached through it, and felt a child's hand grasp his. With the combined effort of the traveler and the friendly person on the other side, he fully opened the door and stepped through it into the City of Memories. Unfortunately, he didn't get a chance to thank the one who assisted him because he began to lose consciousness from exhaustion. Before he lost awareness, the traveler saw the girl. Just as he fell asleep, he heard her say, "It's okay. You can rest now."

What seemed like several days later, the traveler opened his eyes and saw the girl sitting next to him. "Where was I? That was no memory. Why did that place put me through so much?" the traveler asked of the girl.

With a slight nod, the girl said, "Remember that each door does not only lead you to memories but also unresolved emotional states that need to be acknowledged. Emotions are powerful teachers. Listen to them, and you will likely find the answers to the questions that you are asking. Even when something meaningful ends, we should not think that an ending has nothing to teach us."

The traveler hesitated and then asked the girl, "What do you mean?"

She responded, "When something ends, allow yourself to feel its loss, but do not mourn its leaving. Rather, appreciate that what it taught you will cast out seeds, which will enact new growth that wouldn't have occurred otherwise. For love never leaves us. It is regenerative."

The traveler grinned slightly, and the door he had just entered changed from purple to a bright sky blue as he did. He breathed deeply and felt a peace reside within him as he felt thanks for having withstood his ordeal. "Thank you," he said to the girl. She nodded, smiling back at him, and then they enjoyed the settled silence that followed. "Well, I suppose I should see if any other doors need exploring. I will keep your words in mind, Friend."

"Good. Until next time," the girl responded.

With that, the traveler rested for the night, and prepared for more explorations.

XIV
The Glass Piano

When the traveler awoke, the girl was gone. However, her words floated freely in his memory. He noted the sensation and then proceeded to get up and walk into the city streets. After turning a corner, the traveler listened for any doors that might be calling out to him. However, instead, the traveler heard a gentle melody playing in the distance. It was softly but fervently beckoning him. He followed the song, which thickly saturated the air the closer he got to its source, and noticed that it was leading to the edge of the City of Memories.

Finally, having followed the melody to its source, he was astonished to find a sight he had never seen before. A musician sat at a piano that was wholly unique to the traveler. In fact, he could hardly even see the piano until he got closer to it. This piano, this fascinating instrument, was completely transparent! With eyes and mouth noticeably agape, the musician smiled and chuckled at the traveler. "What...what is that?" asked the traveler.

The musician responded, "Well, hello to you. No need for introductions, it seems, hmmm?"

"Oh, my apologies. I am simply a traveler exploring the city."

"A traveler? Yes, you have the look of a traveler in your eyes. I have seen a similar quiet fervency in the gaze of other travelers, too."

The traveler smiled, and they both shared a quiet moment as they watched each other.

"Well, traveler, to answer your question, I am Holsih Ollegsta, a musician. I play what comes to me on this piano, and this piano is my instrument of choice. It is a glass piano," Holsih responded.

As Holsih played a few notes, the traveler's ears perked up at the clarity and ping of each. The music that reverberated from the glass piano was truly remarkable.

"What is that piece you are playing?" asked the traveler.

Holsih responded, "A melody of the wind that comes from the surrounding mountains. They come from a higher elevation, a place that inspires me greatly. I refer to these melodies as accumulations of the sky because I write them utilizing the sky mountains."

The traveler shook his head in a confused manner and said, "Sky mountains? What…"

Holsih continued, "What are sky mountains? Look up."

The traveler did just so and saw a sky full of brilliantly sunlit clouds.

"I…I've never seen such beautiful clouds before," the traveler stated quietly, almost to himself. As he said those words, the clouds began to change rapidly from stratified and layered to soft and elongated. Startled, the traveler took a step back at the sudden shift in the shape of the clouds. Holsih beamed, noting his reaction. Suddenly, the clouds transformed again, shifting into almost jagged shapes that seemed to reflect the traveler's feelings of surprise and angst. "Why are they doing that?" asked the traveler. He started to smile as he noticed the clouds widening, becoming more fluffy and rounded. The traveler, astonished, next asked, "They…are they responding…to me?"

Holsih said, "They are responding to us both. These sky mountains are excellent listeners and mirrors of their environment. What is really causing them to behave in this manner though, are the emotions we are experiencing while playing the glass piano here."

Holsih played a bit more, and as the traveler felt his feelings rise, the clouds continued to respond to each emotional shift. Each note was so rich and full of sound that the traveler felt he could almost pluck each melody out of the air and admire them as he would a stunning piece of jewelry.

"Tell me, Traveler, which clouds are most interesting to you?" asked Holsih. The traveler, fully transfixed, sat beside the glass piano and stared at the sky mountains. "Traveler. What words come to mind when you look at the sky mountains?" Holsih inquired. The traveler took several moments before responding and offered several words that carried their own emotional weight. "Now, find a note for each word that you stated that best describes the feeling that emerges."

A bit perplexed, the traveler paused but, feeling curious, got up and walked over to the glass piano. Holsih scooted down the glass bench, making room for the traveler next to him. One by one, the traveler thought about each word and the feelings they elicited from him. Pushing several keys down, he found notes that fit each feeling like a glove. Eventually, the traveler composed an emotive melody that mirrored his current emotional state. A small grin emerged on the traveler's face as he played the finished song, and the sky mountains danced with joy. Taking a moment to appreciate the melody, the traveler lowered his hands onto his lap.

"That is a fine song. What made you think of these words and notes, and what emotions drove this melody?"

Almost without hesitation, the traveler said, "I felt the love of my family. My home. I thought of everyone that I have ever cared for and what they mean to me. Though they are not near me, they are with me in my heart."

Holsih stated, "Very meaningful. What is the name of this piece?"

The traveler responded with a single word, spoken in such a quiet tone that it was almost imperceptible to Holsih.

Smiling, Holsih stated, "That is a good name. It suits this piece. Thank you for sharing that with me. This is why I play the glass piano. To learn from and connect with emotional reflections from travelers. Even disparate parts of ourselves are not so unrelated to each other, hmmm?"

The Traveler chuckled slightly and responded by extending his hand. Holsih returned the gesture by reaching out his own, and the two shook hands.

"Thank you as well. I appreciate this music lesson," the traveler said.

After nodding his head in reciprocal appreciation, Holsih turned his gaze to the horizon beyond the City of Memories.

"There is a place that you might want to explore just a few miles from here. It's near the mountain just ahead," Holsih said.

"I've never been there before. Seems like a good day for exploring, though."

"Well said."

"What is this place that you speak of? What should I look for there?" the traveler asked.

"It's a small town. You will likely find some interesting insights there."

"Thank you. I'll stay the night in the city and then head there in the morning." The traveler smiled, making Holsih chuckle in return.

"Okay. Be well, Friend."

With a nod, the traveler got up from the glass bench. He returned to the City of Memories to rest for the night before his next journey.

XV
The Library of Living Books

The sandy ground crunched under the traveler's feet as he made his way to the unknown city. Birds chirped as a wistful song brought a sense of wanderlust and a craving for settling. Feeling the gritty traction of the ground against his feet, the traveler climbed hills and traversed valleys while a thirst welled up in his mouth. "I am tired...so tired...yet I must go on," said the traveler. His eyes burned as he blinked refreshing moisture over them.

Suddenly, a gentle smell made its way to the traveler's nose. "Freshly baked bread, and...tea," the traveler said in an undertone. His mouth watered, and tears escaped. Making it to the top of a small hill, the traveler finally saw the source of these aromas. "A town. I've made it!" His senses beckoned him to a small cottage bakery. "Hello? Is someone there?" the traveler asked upon reaching the front counter of the bakery.

Footsteps emerged from a far-off room and slowly made their way to the traveler. "Yes, lad, I hear you, I hear you. Just a moment," the baker said. He looked over at the traveler and exclaimed, "Oh, hello Traveler, welcome to Lib Town. So nice of you to call in. Is this your first time here?"

The traveler slumped into a chair at the front counter and responded, "Yes, I am looking for something, someplace, but I am so thirsty and hungry."

The baker smiled and said, "Oh, but you are famished and thirsty! I can see it in your eyes. I have just the thing."

Rushing into the back room, the baker soon returned with a tray of freshly baked bread, a small container of butter, a cup of water, and some hot tea, placing everything in front of the traveler. The smell and sight of these items brought tears to the traveler's eyes.

"It's been a long journey, and I am so tired."

"It seems that you got here just in time. I just pulled these out of the oven, and they are still hot. Come, come, have some, I insist."

First, taking a sip of water, the traveler noticed it was refreshing spring water. A smile rose to his face. After putting the cup down, he reached for the tea. The traveler felt his mind almost sigh with relief as he took his first sip. The traveler felt his strength returning. The tea tasted like summer on his tongue. The taste was sweet, the fragrance was floral, and the sensation warmed his throat.

"I know this taste. Where did you get the water for this tea?" the traveler inquired.

The baker responded, "Oh, well, I harvested it from a nearby spring by an old ravine once said to be home to an oasis. That was some time ago, and I can't confirm its authenticity, but it's a nice story nonetheless. The water speaks for itself, in any case. The minerals have proven very healing to the villagers of this town. The only strange thing is that the ravine had this odd gate in what used to be an open field, and some old bones of a large animal were located there. It looked like a bull or cow, but we weren't sure. All we know is that stories abound about that place, and the water is absolutely rejuvenating. It makes for delicious afternoon tea."

The traveler smiled, nodded, and said, "It's some of the best tea I have ever tasted. Thank you."

After several nourishing pieces of bread with butter, the traveler began feeling like himself again.

"Well, surely you will want to explore our town," the baker said.

"Yes, I would, but I'm not sure where to start. What do you recommend?"

"Well, most people visit the tea and chocolate shops. However, there is one place that you must visit. The library."

The traveler's ears instinctively perked up upon hearing those last two words. "The library?" the traveler inquired.

"Yes, it's quite old, and many people often find answers to their questions by scanning the pages of the books that are collected there."

The traveler almost intuitively felt that this was where he needed to go. First, however, he needed to regain his strength.

"Is there a place to stay for the night?"

"Why Lad, this bakery has a few extra rooms for boarders to stay as needed. Shall I prepare a room for you?"

"That would be fine. Just fine, thank you."

—————

Waking up with refreshed body, mind, and heart, the traveler went downstairs to greet the baker. The baker, face dusted with flour, exchanged pleasantries.

"So, where is the library that you mentioned yesterday?"

"It's located at the end of Downtown Lib. It's not hard to find as it has a book sign right above the door," replied the baker.

"Thank you. I will take some of that delicious bread and butter with me. Is there any of it left?"

"Of course. Here you are. May your journey bring you peace and lots of joy."

They both nodded kindly to each other, and the traveler went outside to explore the town. The traveler took several deep breaths in and out as he saw life happening around him. Children, parents, and young couples interacted around him. Each was writing their own story by living their lives. Every breath seemed an affirmation of life, and each exhale acted as a confirmation of moving forward. Looking far ahead, the traveler saw the library. As he walked up to it, he paused for a moment before heading inside.

Books. Everywhere there were books. Innumerable subjects lay before the traveler, waiting to be asked what life was ready to convey next and what of life had happened already. They waited to convey lessons to any and all waiting readers. The traveler felt a heaviness in his chest, wanting to read them all, but then let it go, realizing that life would do the teaching. All he had to do was open his mind to what lessons found him. Oddly, as the traveler passed one aisle, he saw a spiderweb being gently blown by a breeze in the corner.

"That's odd," said the traveler.

Walking up to the web, he placed his hand next to it and felt a coldness hit it. There was something behind the bookcase, but what? Lightly pushing up against the shelves, he felt the entire case move slightly.

"A false wall?" the traveler exclaimed inquisitively.

The traveler pushed more fervently, revealing more and more of a passageway behind the shelves until it was fully exposed. The corridor was well-lit, but so as not to cause any alarm or unnecessary suspicion, the traveler closed the bookcase behind him and began traversing the passageway.

————

After some time of walking, the traveler reached a door that had script he couldn't translate across it. It was ancient by the looks of it, which only added to the traveler's curiosity. He slowly but fervently pushed open the door and was shocked by what he saw on the other side. There were volumes upon volumes of books in perfect condition, yet the bookcases holding them seemed old beyond time itself. He chose one of the books, opened it, and found the following title on the front cover, *The Library of Living Books: Holsih Ollegsta.*

"Wait, that's the musician that I met back in the City of Memories. Why is his name on this book in another town?" the traveler inquired.

The traveler opened the book and was surprised to find the life of Ollegsta was written on its pages. Skipping ahead to the end of the book, he realized that the pages were blank. Finding this strange, the traveler flipped backward through the book until he found where the text stopped within the book. There, he found something that shocked him further. The last page or two chronicled the traveler's meeting with Holsih. Every detail was there.

"What? The text stopped where my interaction with Holsih ended," exclaimed The traveler.

Slowly, an inner awareness, perhaps even a remembering, began to unfold within the traveler's mind. Shaking his head gently, he put the book away and continued exploring. The traveler slowly opened and read book after book, all titled with the names of people he had met. The names of his loved ones, friends, and even people he hadn't met were there in the Living Library. A bright light illuminated above a box at the library's center. Walking up to the box, he noticed a book rested inside of it. Upon reading the name on the cover, the traveler's eyes widened.

"That's...that's my name," he said in an undertone.

Slowly picking it up, the traveler read through the book and was amazed that it told the story of the boy—his younger self.

"This is my story. My life," said the traveler.

Tears welled up in his eyes as he recounted the boy's struggles with the lonely one, the open field, the Falling Forest, and his own interactions with him. The traveler reached a section in the book where he had met the boy once again and, eventually, where they went on their own paths. Everything was there. Flipping ahead, the traveler went to the last page with text and found where he was currently. Text slowly filled the page where he had found this library. The words "The Living Library" were written at various points on the page. Suddenly, everything began to click within the mind of the traveler.

"I know where I am. I know why I am here."

The traveler put the book back into the box and ran through the aisles of bookcases, scanning each of the hardbacks on them. The traveler realized the Living Library is where he could go to reflect more concretely on his collections of experiences. Here, he could digest the lessons he had learned and sound them down into his heart. Suddenly, next to him, the traveler felt the presence of an old friend—one who never was far off from him.

"Hello, old friend," a voice said; it was the lonely one, the boy, the traveler's heart standing next to him.

"I knew that you were never far off from me. I knew that you would return," the traveler said.

Smiling, the traveler turned and saw a beautiful young woman. She had the voice and appearance of both the girl and the woman intertwined into one. She embraced him with such warmth that the traveler felt his heart almost burst from the overflow of emotion that swelled inside him.

"Yes, you remember now that I told you. We are never far from one another. When you need me, I will help you find your way," his heart said.

Book by book, she reminded the traveler of all who cared for him and then showed him countless other books without names.

"What are these?" the traveler asked his heart.

She responded, "These, dear friend, are the many more you have yet to meet who will fill you with their stories and lessons which will become part of you. Do you see now? You are part of something much bigger than yourself. You are multitudes of voices and people. Their experiences will fill and inform your own. No matter where you go, know that it will be ready for you whenever you need to return to this place. Above all else, know that we love you," his heart said.

Feeling warmth fill him up, he remembered why he embarked on this journey. He wanted to affirm that he could learn and grow regardless of where he went. This library was just that. With a smile, he looked at his heart, and she grasped both his hands.

She said, "Your journey within is just beginning. It never ends, really. It only ends when you stop affirming life. You and the boy are the same, and you both will always be connected. Adult and child are just figments and constructs of the mind. After all, adults are, at their core, children searching for and finding home. All the people that you feel left you are not gone entirely. When perceived with the heart, a goodbye is only a separation with what is seen, not with memories and love. They all live through your love for them."

Looking around the Living Library, the traveler's eyes welled up with tears, and he sobbed warm tears of heartfelt thanks. His heart extended open their arms, embracing the traveler, and said, "Never forget. We are always here with you."

With that, his heart returned within him. As he left the Living Library, the traveler smiled and thanked everyone and their stories that informed his heart. Upon leaving, he noticed that the entrance to the Living Library was no longer behind a closed bookcase but rather was now a visible door. It was ready for the traveler to access at any time.

———

As he left the library of Lib Town, he smiled upon entering the open street and saw all the people around him. The traveler recognized them all. They were all memories of people that he knew or had met. Smiling to himself, the traveler returned to the bakery and spoke with the baker.

"It seems you found some answers, yes?" the baker asked.

"Yes, many more questions too, but ones that I know will inform me for future journeys," the traveler said.

"Glad to hear, Lad. I know that you will be embarking on your next journey, but why don't you take this freshly-baked loaf with you. I call this loaf, 'The Terra Special,'" the baker said.

"Thank you for all of your kindness. Here take these tea leaves. They have healing properties and will serve you well."

"I will take them gladly. Many thanks. Goodnight, Lad. Sleep well."

Nodding appreciatively, the traveler went upstairs, slept, and prepared for his next journey.

XVI
Forest of the Heart

Upon waking the next morning, the traveler readied himself. Before leaving the room, he sat on the bed for a time and analyzed his heart. He asked himself, "Where should I go next? I have traveled to many places, yet I am only truly taking time to get to know who I really am or could be." Sitting for a few more moments, with the morning sun's rays breaking through the window, he felt the warm caress of a new day. However, he also felt the coolness of shadow at his back. "I have much left to do and to learn. But perhaps it is time to return home while I can with my family."

As though by instinct, the traveler looked out the window, and his gaze rested on a dense forest. The exterior was beautiful, but the inside was so thick with darkness and mist that he could not see anything clearly. "That's the forest. The same forest that the boy found near the beginning of his journey. What did he call it? The Falling Forest, I believe." Bringing only his bread, tea, cup, and thermos of boiled water, the traveler went downstairs to embark on his visit to the Falling Forest.

Noticing the traveler in the corner of his eye, the baker said, "Well, good morning, Lad! You look well-rested. Where are you going to go now?"

The traveler cast a gentle gaze at the baker; with a grin, he said, "There's a forest near the outskirts of Lib Town. I visited there many *years* ago and learned some very important lessons while I was there. I would like to visit it again. I am curious how that place has changed with the passing of years."

With a worried expression, the baker responded, "That forest has been there for ages. It is a quiet and isolating place where people go to think and ponder on life. Many who tell me they are going to go there often change their minds. I wondered why that was for many years, until I went in myself. The forest doesn't have all the distractions around that we fill our time with. It gives you time to breathe. When that happens, we often find not only the good and fine things of life, but also the things we often hide from ourselves. The things we might wish that we hadn't found."

The Traveler, intrigued, asked, "What did you find in there?"

With a twinkle in his eyes, the baker responded, "I found that I could process all my pain in those woods. It hurt inside, but after a good cry, and staring into the clouds, I confirmed who I really was in that forest. Hard to explain. You just have to go and find out for yourself."

After thinking for a moment, the traveler smiled and said, "Then that's where I'm going to go. Thank you for your generosity and kindness. I will always remember that. I hope to see you again."

"I have enjoyed our conversation. I don't like to say 'goodbye', as I hope that I will meet people again one day. So for now, I'll just say, brave journey, and until next time, Lad."

With a good-natured smile, the traveler said, "I will look forward to it. Until next time."

With that, the traveler opened the door, and let the sounds of life fill his senses. Saying goodbye to everyone in Lib Town almost felt somber, but also it filled this heart with joy knowing that life would continue for everyone. People living, having children, raising families, making bread, helping one another to grow, and sharing lessons from generation to generation. He was glad to be part of it for as long as he could. However, for now, he made his way to the Falling Forest.

———

As the traveler reached the forest's outer edge, he thought he might turn back. The shadows seemed so dense inside that it made his heart skip a beat. However, he felt a strong urge to continue moving forward. So gathering his courage, the traveler began walking into the forest. The darkness blurred his vision and made everything appear the same. Nothing was clear cut, and the animals seemed angry at his presence.

Feeling overwhelmed, the traveler decided to take a moment to collect his thoughts. He sat down, opened his bag, and pulled out his thermos of boiling water, cup, and tea. Placing a flat tree bark slab in front of him, the traveler set up his teawares on it and began preparing tea. He inhaled deeply as he poured the boiled water into his cup to warm it. Pouring the water out, he gently took a long breath out and opened the container of tea leaves. He quietly poured some of the dark and earthly sweet leaves into his cup. As he poured water over the tea leaves, the aroma seemed to fill the forest around him.

With each inhalation, the darkness and mist in the forest seemed to fall and fade all around him, revealing patches of light through the trees. Picking up the cup and bringing it under his nose, the traveler took a deep breath in, and the aroma wrapped him in warmth that filled his entire being. With the first sip, his insides fully relaxed and began accepting the darkness around him. Then, out of nowhere, the traveler heard a gentle and familiar voice.

It said, "Hello, dear friend. Are you ready? Are you ready to find home?"

Opening his eyes, the traveler smiled, seeing his old friend, the lonely one, in front of him. However, his heart didn't look as lonely anymore. She was bathed in light and emanated a warmth that he had never seen or felt before.

She said, "As long as you remember that home is always within you, no darkness can isolate you completely from life. However, there is something that you must readily admit to yourself, first."

With inquiring eyes, he asked her, "What is it?"

"These shadows around you, you must learn to integrate them."

After a moment of pause, he said, "Why? Why would I want to integrate what I cannot see?"

With a serious expression, his heart said, "Many people want to identify only with the good, the known part of themselves. Often, this causes us to split our identity. While it is good to work on the good and positive qualities that we possess, we must also accept and realize that the opposite exists within us as well. Otherwise, we cannot fully accept our entire being. To disown what the negative experiences have taught us is to ignore what the challenges in life have taught us. When we see something perceived as bad in others, and it makes us emotionally charged, that is a sign of what we are suppressing or not accepting is part of us. Look for that and face it."

With a slightly tired expression, the traveler said, "How do I do that?" Looking beyond his heart, everything around the traveler had become blurry and hard to perceive. Shaking his head a bit, the traveler remembered the words of his heart. "Accept and face it," he echoed out loud.

With another sip of his tea, he noticed one of the wild animals started walking toward him. It was a wolf. The wolf noticed the traveler staring in its direction and began to snarl and growl. Swallowing audibly, the traveler held his gaze, and almost without hesitation, the wolf began snarling louder and drew closer. Holding his gaze still, the traveler steadied his breath and noticed the wolf running toward him at full speed with its jaws opened wide.

With a moment that seemed to last for times untold and also an instant, the traveler held out his cup of tea to the wolf as it neared him. Right before the wolf reached the traveler, it stopped just in front of him. The wolf snarled and acted like it was curious about what the traveler would do next. The traveler thought about the boy and that nothing is ever as it seems on the surface. Even ferocious beings can simply be parts of us that need acceptance in order to grow.

"It's okay. You are safe here. Thank you for protecting what needed protecting. I know that you meant well. I am not your enemy, and you are not mine. Sometimes, things don't go the way we wanted, but often, they worked out the way they really should have." The wolf smelled the air near the traveler, and its snarl slowly quieted to a few small whimpers. Holding his cup of tea out to the wolf, the traveler asked, "Would you like some tea? Would you like to come home?"

The wolf sat for a moment and then howled for several seconds. Meeting the gaze of the traveler, the wolf approached the cup extended out in front of him and began to lap up the warm tea. The traveler felt the weight of the wolf's chin on the cup as it drank the tea. After drinking the entire cup, the wolf stepped over to the traveler and gently licked his face.

Meeting the wolf's gaze, the traveler said, "Thank you for holding the pain. So much is lost in life, but so much is also gained. The memories of loved ones can live again through our actions and the love we show others. We may be angry when they leave us, but that love is renewable and everlasting. Anger is never meant to be held onto; the boy taught me that. We have to let anger go." With that, the wolf laid down, set its head on the traveler's lap, and gave a deep sigh. "I accept you. I accept that you were doing what you felt was right in the moment. Thank you."

With that, the wolf closed its eyes and slept. After a few moments, the traveler felt a tear. Shutting his eyes, and then reopening them, the forest was no longer blurry or in complete darkness but showed vivid colors lit by the sun. Suddenly, the wolf was no longer by his side. He breathed in the memory of the wolf, which felt like a fall breeze. It smelled like a change of seasons, a coldness shifting into warmness on the skin. Then the traveler's heart was there, next to him.

"Thank you," the traveler said to his heart.

"You have done well," she responded, adding, "The wolf that you first encountered was all the heartache that the boy had held within himself. At first, you ran from it, unsure what it would do to you. When you finally faced it, it could reveal itself as simply a part of you that needed acknowledgment. However, you hadn't faced all of it on your own. The boy could only show you so much. You had to really sit and accept what was left of the anger, fear, and opposing forces within you that needed to be understood. You gave thanks to it for protecting you, but that you were now ready to accept the parts of yourself that you didn't want to face."

The traveler's heart continued to share, saying, "Your journey is just beginning, though. The next time you are faced with these strong emotions, you will be more ready to take them on. Remember that you used to call this place the Falling Forest? The actual name of this place is Forest of the Heart. It reflects your mind and heart, and who you are. It is the place your mind and heart go for healing, which rests between the state of being asleep and awake. I will always be there to help when you need me. Are you ready to awaken?"

Feeling more whole, the traveler set his gaze ahead and nodded to his heart. After cleaning his teaware, he inhaled deeply, closed his eyes, exhaled deeply, and then opened his eyes. Though his heart was no longer in front of him, he knew she would always be with him. As he put his teaware away, the traveler's vision slowly cleared. With that, he began walking through the forest.

As the onset of sunset began, the traveler neared the edge of the opposite side of the forest. What he saw upon exiting the forest surprised him. He had returned to the City of Memories! There to greet him were the girl and the woman. They were there extending their hands out to him.

"Are you ready to begin your journey home?" they asked.

For a moment, he thought back on all the people he had met and those he had yet to meet. He knew it was time to continue his journey home.

"Rest before continuing your journey, Friend," the girl and the woman said.

Nodding his head in agreement, the traveler entered the city and stayed overnight, preparing for his journey.

XVII
Fingerprints on the Heart

Sleep found the traveler once he entered the City of Memories. The girl and the woman kindly gave him shelter. They brought him through a door, which led to a memory of one of his favorite place—his bedroom. He had spent many an hour pondering, sleeping, and waking, all while he readied himself for what each day would bring. With a tired feeling in his heart, he laid down in his bed, and felt his eyelids grow heavy. He slept, he dreamt of home, and he rested.

As the traveler lulled in the spaces between being asleep and awake, he suddenly opened his eyes. His body gently perceived something – a memory emerging. He sniffed the air and noticed his mouth began to water. He pondered on this strong reaction and realized he knew the scent that lingered in his memory. Quickly getting dressed, he left his room, and walked outside. The smell was becoming more intense. The traveler walked farther, following the fragrance.

He gazed ahead and saw a door he had never perceived before. It looked familiar, yet he couldn't quite place where he had seen it. As he approached the door, the smell that drew him from his room became incredibly potent. Reaching for the door, he grasped the knob, turned it, and it slowly opened. All at once, the fragrances that encompassed all that was good in his life warmly surrounded him. He looked inside the door and immediately recognized where he was.

"My childhood home," the traveler said.

As he walked through the entryway, he slowly made his way to the kitchen. It was there that he found the source of the meaningful scent. He gazed onward, and his eyes began to water with many emotions. His grandmother was there in front of him, making one of his favorite foods.

"Mijo. Oh, Mijo!" his grandmother said upon noticing him standing there.

"Hi, Grandmama."Almost falling into her, they embraced one another in a moment that transcended time. "Grandmama, I have missed you so much. I never thought I would see you again," he said as tears ran down his cheek.

She stared into his eyes and said, "Ya, ya, now. No, don't cry. You need to eat, yes? You are tired, my poor Mijo. Sit here with me. I made buñuelos, and you must eat."

Nodding in agreement, he sat at the table in the kitchen, and his grandmother served him his favorite treat. The smell reminded him of good and bad times, lessons learned, and many still being learned.

The traveler saw the plate full of steaming hot buñuelos in front of him. They smelled of fried pastry, cinnamon, and sugar. He lifted the treat to his mouth, took a long whiff, and then a big bite. The texture and the taste immediately reminded him of everything wonderful in his life. He remembered all he had met and who had left him in his life, all he had let go of and felt thankful for. The taste opened his heart, and for the first time in many years, he felt at peace, even if for just a moment. He chewed, he ruminated, and he laughed within himself. He smiled and felt at home.

"Thank you, Grandmama. Thank you for everything you taught me, and continue to teach me through your lessons. Every day, I miss you and think of how much you feel love for so many. You never pretended to be more than who you are. I am working on finding that path within myself. I am at peace with that path now. Every day, I realize that. We cannot be unless we know what we stand for, who we love, and why. The reasons change; they shift and find new faces, new people to settle into. In time, maybe I will do so like you."

"Mijo, I love you. I am proud of who you have become. That is all that I want for you. Be happy."

Gazing down at the plate of buñuelos, the traveler swallowed hard and said, "I am that more and less at times. However, I will never forget that all things pass. Nothing good or bad is forever. It all keeps moving and driving forward. Best to appreciate it and be thankful for what it has to teach you now. I love you."

After eating several buñuelos, the traveler stood up and hugged his grandmother.

"I will always remember this feeling. It will guide me whenever I forget. Thank you."

After hugging her, he noticed a door at the far edge of the room. Wiping moister from his eyes and cinnamon from his mouth, he bid her farewell. Tears rushed to her eyes as she embraced him one more time. Clearing his throat, the traveler closed his eyes and squeezed her back. He let go of her hand and began walking to the door. He stopped, listened to her cooking for just a moment more, and then walked through the door.

A bright light emerged through the other side of the door, and what he saw there brought a smile to his face.

"Hello, old friend," the traveler said.

"Welcome back, old friend," the boy responded.

"You are ready, aren't you?"

"Yes. Let's go home."

Looking into the room, the traveler and the boy noticed two red chairs facing one another. Grasping hands, they walked to the chairs, and each sat on one.

"Home. Let's go home," the traveler said.

He closed his eyes, took a deep breath, and allowed warmth to fill him up inside.

As the traveler opens his eyes, he notices he is back in his room, not the one from his childhood or from any other time, but his current home. It is a winter morning, yet the cold in the air does not cause him to fall into a saddened state. He reaches over and turns on a lamp near his bedside. His phone dings, having just received a text. His friends invite him to join them for a meal in a few hours.

He smiles and responds, typing, "Sounds great. See you then."

He wipes sleep away from his eyes, and feels his body relax after a good night's sleep. The traveler checks the calendar on his phone and stretches. Slowly, he wakens from his dream. Though he begins to forget the specifics of his journey, as the moments pass, an unconscious reminder causes him to smile. He recalls the image of blue thread as he shakes off the last vestiges of sleepiness. People and places begin to shimmer in the deep recesses of his mind; the warmth of their love fills his heart. Though separated, they are never apart. These unconscious lessons plant themselves deep within an ever-growing mind and heart. Dreams are often subtle ways our minds digest lessons that stretch across decades and even lifetimes. Walking to the window, the traveler looks at the future in action and takes a moment to appreciate the present. Feeling content, he gets ready to meet with his friends—his family—for they have all touched his heart. They have all left their fingerprints on his heart.

Acknowledgments

Thank you to my editorial and production team: Britt Nunes and Allie Kat. Your collective experience and guidance proved truly helpful in fine-tuning this book. You both helped me approach this project with new eyes and more focused intention. You both inspire me to continue writing and learning from my own interior stories, as well as the stories of countless others.

Deep thanks to Dan and Lucinda Kasser. You both taught me to search for questions with intention, and find heartfelt answers to inspire deeper inquiry.

Many thanks to Monika Meler. Your support and friendship have always spurred me forward to challenge myself and grow as an artist, author, and human being.

A meaningful and heartfelt thanks to Jill Vasileff. You taught me to see facing fear as something to challenge my comfort zone. Growth does, indeed, rest on the other side of fear.

A resounding thank you to Merrill Schleier. You taught me to explore and question whatever challenges me most. I am thankful that you inspired me to delve deeper into learning from my intuition and listening to my inner voice.

Much thanks to Trent Burkett. You taught me that there are several solutions to every problem, and that we are stronger than we realize. Above all else, you helped me to appreciate that we can always learn from every version of ourselves across life's journey.

A resonating thanks to Karl Burkheimer. You taught me the importance of becoming a more advanced version of myself. We learn so much from every version of ourselves.

Deep and appreciative thanks to Dylan Beck. You helped me to search and find answers where I feel most uncomfortable, because it will help me find meaningful answers.

Enthusiastic thanks to Jim Koudelka. You taught me to better trust myself, and my artist's intuition. You have helped so many, and I am thankful to have been one of them.

Warmest thanks to Siri Schillios. Your listening ear and kind manner continue to inspire me to this day. I will always remember how much you impacted my life and the lives of so many with your sincerity.

Full and heartfelt thank to Geo Nehl. You taught me the importance of opening my heart and mind through the act of listening. We always have something to learn from each person and their unique life.

To everyone who impacted the writing of this book, too innumerable to count, thank you for being part of my life.